MRS PEPPERPOT
MINDS THE BABY

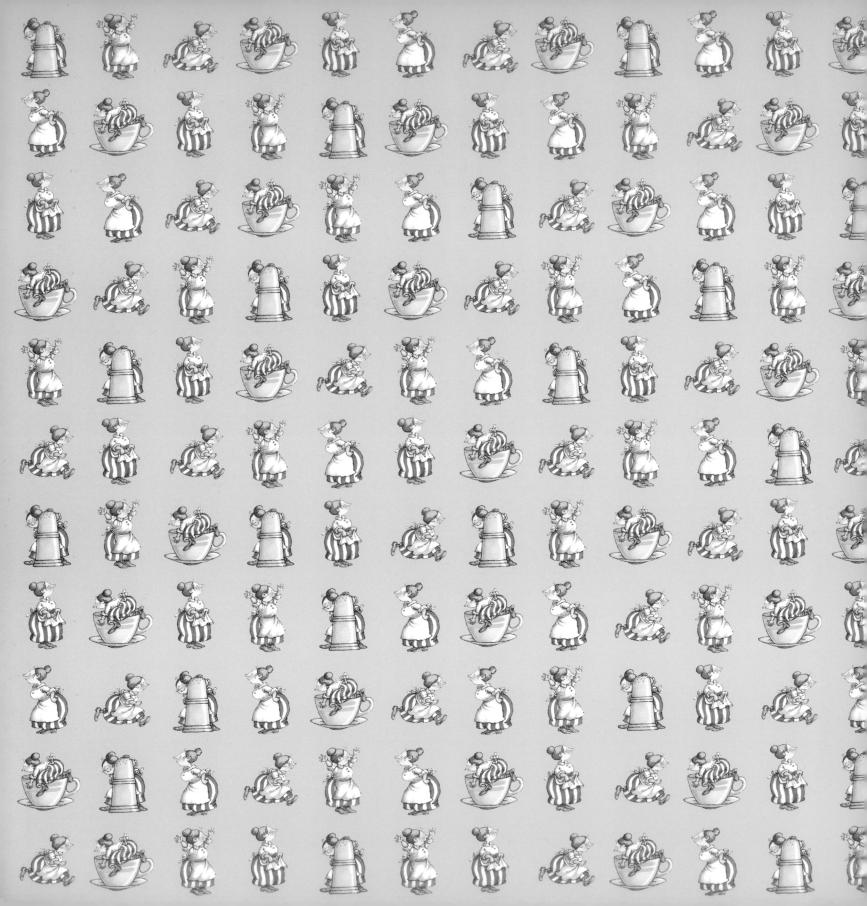

MRS PEPPERPOT MINDS THE BABY
A RED FOX BOOK 978 1 849 41864 5

First published in Great Britain by Hutchinson,
an imprint of Random House Children's Publishers UK
A Random House Group Company

Hutchinson edition published 1960
This Red Fox edition published 2013

1 3 5 7 9 10 8 6 4 2

Red Fox Books are published by Random House Children's Publishers UK,
61– 63 Uxbridge Road, London W5 5SA

www.**randomhousechildrens**.co.uk
www.**randomhouse**.co.uk

Addresses for companies within The Random House Group Limited can be found at:
www.randomhouse.co.uk/offices.htm

THE RANDOM HOUSE GROUP Limited Reg. No. 954009

A CIP catalogue record for this book is available from the British Library.

Printed in China

The Random House Group Limited supports The Forest Stewardship Council (FSC®), the leading
international forest certification organisation. Our books carrying the FSC label are printed on FSC® certified paper.
FSC is the only forest certification scheme endorsed by the leading environmental organisations, including Greenpeace.
Our paper procurement policy can be found at www.randomhouse.co.uk/environment

MRS PEPPERPOT
MINDS THE BABY

ALF PRØYSEN ❖ **HILDA OFFEN**

RED FOX

Let me tell you what happened the day Mrs Pepperpot was asked to mind the baby. She was tidying the house when suddenly there was a knock at the door.

In the porch stood her neighbour with her little boy on her arm. "Forgive me for knocking," she said. "You see, I simply have to go shopping in the town today. I can't take Roger and there's no one in the house to look after him."

"Oh, that's all right!" said Mrs Pepperpot. "I'll look after your little boy."

"You don't need to give him a meal," said the lady. "I've brought some apples for him, for when he starts sucking his fingers."

"Very well," said Mrs Pepperpot, and put the apples in a dish.

The lady said goodbye and Mrs Pepperpot set the baby down on the rug in the sitting room. Then she went out into the kitchen to fetch her broom to start sweeping up. At that very moment she SHRANK!

"Oh dear! Oh dear! Whatever shall I do?" she wailed, for of course now she was much smaller than the baby.

I must go and see what that little fellow is doing, she thought, as she climbed over the doorstep into the sitting room.

Not a moment too soon! For Roger had crawled right across the floor and was just about to pull the tablecloth off the table, together with a pot of jam, a loaf of bread and a big jug of coffee!

Mrs Pepperpot lost no time. She looked about her and pushed over a large silver cup which was standing on the floor, waiting to be polished. The cup made a booming noise as it fell so the baby turned round and started crawling towards it.

"That's right," said Mrs Pepperpot, "you play with that; at least you can't break it."

But Roger wasn't after the silver cup.

Gurgling, "Wan' dolly! Wan' dolly!" he made a bee-line for Mrs Pepperpot, and before she could get away, he had grabbed her by the waist!

He jogged her up and down, and every time Mrs Pepperpot kicked and wriggled to get free, he laughed, "'Ickle,'ickle!" for she was tickling his hand with her feet.

"Let go! Let go!" yelled Mrs Pepperpot.

But Roger was used to his daddy shouting, "Let's go!" when he threw him up in the air and caught him again.

So Roger shouted, "Leggo! Leggo!" and threw the little old woman up in the air with all the strength of his short arms.

Mrs Pepperpot went up and up – nearly to the ceiling!
Luckily she landed on the sofa, but she bounced over and
over before she could stop.

By the time she had caught her breath Roger had found a
pot of ink and was trying to open it.

Mrs Pepperpot had to think very quickly indeed.
"Careful!" she cried. Luckily she found a nut in the sofa and
threw it at Roger, making him turn round.

He dropped the ink pot and started crawling towards the sofa. "Wan' dolly! Wan' dolly!" he gurgled.

And now they started a very funny game of
hide-and-seek – at least it was fun for Roger,
but not for poor old Mrs Pepperpot.

In the end she managed to climb onto the sideboard.

"Aha, you can't catch me now!" she said, feeling much safer.

But then the baby started back towards the ink pot.

"No, no, no!" shouted Mrs Pepperpot.

Roger took no notice. So she put her back against a flowerpot and gave it a push. It fell to the floor with a crash.

Straight away Roger left the ink pot for this new mess of earth and bits of broken flowerpot. He buried both his hands in it and started putting it in his mouth, gurgling, "Nice din-din!"

"No, no, no!" shouted Mrs Pepperpot once more. "Oh, whatever shall I do?"

Her eye caught the apples left by Roger's mother. One after the other she rolled them over the edge of the dish onto the floor.

Roger watched them roll, then he decided to chase them, forgetting his lovely meal of earth. Soon the apples were all over the floor and the baby was crawling happily from one to the other.

Then there was a knock on the door...

"Come in," said Mrs Pepperpot.

Roger's mother opened the door and came in, and there was Mrs Pepperpot as large as life again.

"Has he been naughty?" asked the lady.

"As good as gold," said Mrs Pepperpot. "We've had a high old time together, haven't we, Roger?" And she handed him back to his mother.

"I'll have to take you home now, Precious," said the lady.

But the little fellow began to cry. "Wan' dolly! Wan' dolly!" he sobbed.

"Want dolly?" said his mother. "But you didn't bring a dolly – you don't even have one at home."

She turned to Mrs Pepperpot. "I don't know what he means."

"Oh, children say so many things grown-ups don't understand," said Mrs Pepperpot, and waved goodbye to Roger and his mother.

Then she set about cleaning up her house.

MORE MRS PEPPERPOT BOOKS
FOR YOU TO ENJOY!

MRS PEPPERPOT MINDS THE BABY

A classic story with a touch of magic

ALF PRØYSEN ❖ HILDA OFFEN

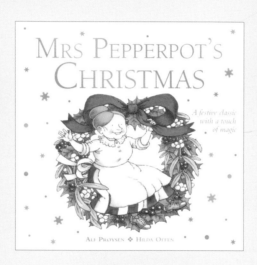

MRS PEPPERPOT'S CHRISTMAS

A festive classic with a touch of magic

ALF PRØYSEN ❖ HILDA OFFEN

MRS PEPPERPOT AT THE BAZAAR

A classic story with a touch of magic

ALF PRØYSEN ❖ HILDA OFFEN

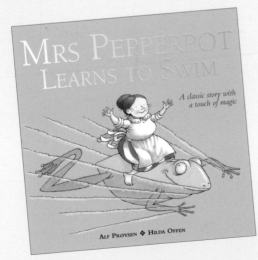

MRS PEPPERPOT LEARNS TO SWIM

A classic story with a touch of magic

ALF PRØYSEN ❖ HILDA OFFEN

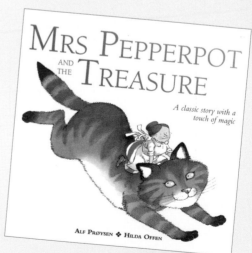

MRS PEPPERPOT AND THE TREASURE

A classic story with a touch of magic

ALF PRØYSEN ❖ HILDA OFFEN